Based on an idea by Frans Hol

First published in the United States, Great Britain, Canada,
Australia, and New Zealand in 2000 by North-South Books,
an imprint of Nord-Süd Verlag AG, Gossau Zürich, Switzerland.

Copyright © 1998 by Hatier Littérature Générale, Paris.
First published in France under the title *La naissance de la lune*.
English translation copyright © 2000 by North-South Books Inc.

Distributed in the United States by North-South Books Inc., New York.

Library of Congress Cataloging-in-Publication Data is available.
A CIP catalogue record for this book is available from The British Library.
ISBN 0-7358-1249-7 (trade binding)
3 5 7 9 TB 10 8 6 4 2
ISBN 0-7358-1250-0 (library binding)
1 3 5 7 9 LB 10 8 6 4 2
Printed in Belgium

For more information about our books,
and the authors and artists who create them,
visit our web site: www.northsouth.com

Coby Hol

The Birth of the Moon

Translated by Sibylle Kazeroid

North-South Books · New York · London

ONCE UPON A TIME it was dark at night
and the animals couldn't see a thing.

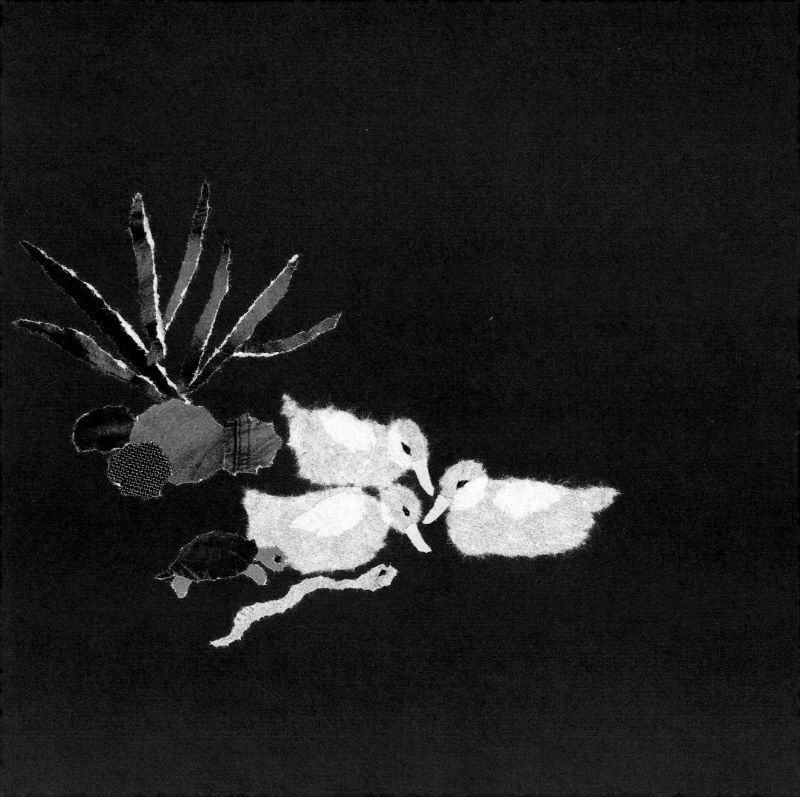

So they asked the sun if he would
shine on them during the night
as well as the day.

"I'm sorry, but I can't," said the sun. "I have to light the other side of the world. When it's night here, it's day there. But I have an idea. Watch the sky tonight. There will be a surprise."

The animals waited impatiently all day long. When night fell, they saw a tiny crescent of light in the sky.

"Bravo!" they cried. "Thank you, Sun!"

The next morning the sun asked the
animals how they liked the surprise.

"It's wonderful!" they replied. "But could
you make the crescent a little bigger?"
"I will try," said the sun.
And that night, the crescent of light
had grown.

Each night the crescent grew
and grew, until it became a
lovely, round full moon.

The animals soon became
used to having light at night.
They didn't marvel at it anymore
and they didn't even think of
thanking the sun.

This made the sun angry.
He made the moon smaller
and smaller, until one night
it completely disappeared.

That night the sky was dark again.

"How ungrateful we were," said the
animals sadly.

The next day they went to apologize to the sun.

"We're sorry," they said. "Please bring back the moon. We can't see at night without it."

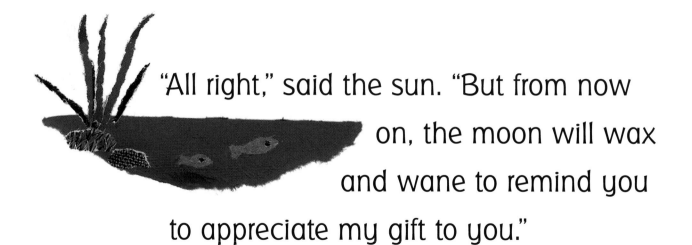

"All right," said the sun. "But from now on, the moon will wax and wane to remind you to appreciate my gift to you."

Ever since then, the moon disappears completely one night a month. But it always returns—sometimes as just a tiny crescent, sometimes as a round full moon—to light the night for the animals.